For Liz,
as we dance ever onward into our dotage.
– M.D.

For the dancer she once was.
– S.J. & L.F.

SIMON AND SCHUSTER
First published in Great Britain in 2005 by Simon & Schuster UK Ltd
Africa House, 64·78 Kingsway, London WC2B 6AH

This paperback edition first published in 2005

Text copyright © 2005 Malachy Doyle
Illustrations copyright © 2005 Steve Johnson and Lou Fancher

The right of Malachy Doyle and Steve Johnson and Lou Fancher to be
identified as the author and illustrators of this work has been asserted by
them in accordance with the Copyright, Designs and Patents Act, 1988

Book designed by Lou Fancher
The text for this book is set in Nicolas·Jensen
The illustrations are rendered in oil on paper

A CIP catalogue record for this book is available from the British Library upon request

ISBN 0·689·87310·7

Printed in China
1 3 5 7 9 10 8 6 4 2

The DANCING TIGER

by **Malachy Doyle**

paintings by **Steve Johnson** and **Lou Fancher**

SIMON AND SCHUSTER

London • New York • Sydney

There's a quiet, gentle tiger
In the woods below the hill,
And he dances on his tiptoes,
When the world is dreaming, still.

So you only ever hear him
In the silence of the night.
And you only ever see him
When the full moon's shining bright.

One summer night I saw him first,
Twirling, whirling round.
And then I heard him gasp in fright –
He knew that he'd been found.

As he turned to me and whispered,
'Please don't mention that I'm here.'
The laughter in his lightning eyes
Swept away my fear.

'*I*f you will keep me secret,
And never tell a soul,
Then you may come and dance with me
On nights the moon is whole.'

So once a month, from then till now,
I've tiptoed to the wood.
We've swirled and swayed among the trees,
As Tiger said we could.

We've skipped in spring through bluebells,

*I*n summer circled slow,

We've high-kicked in the autumn leaves,

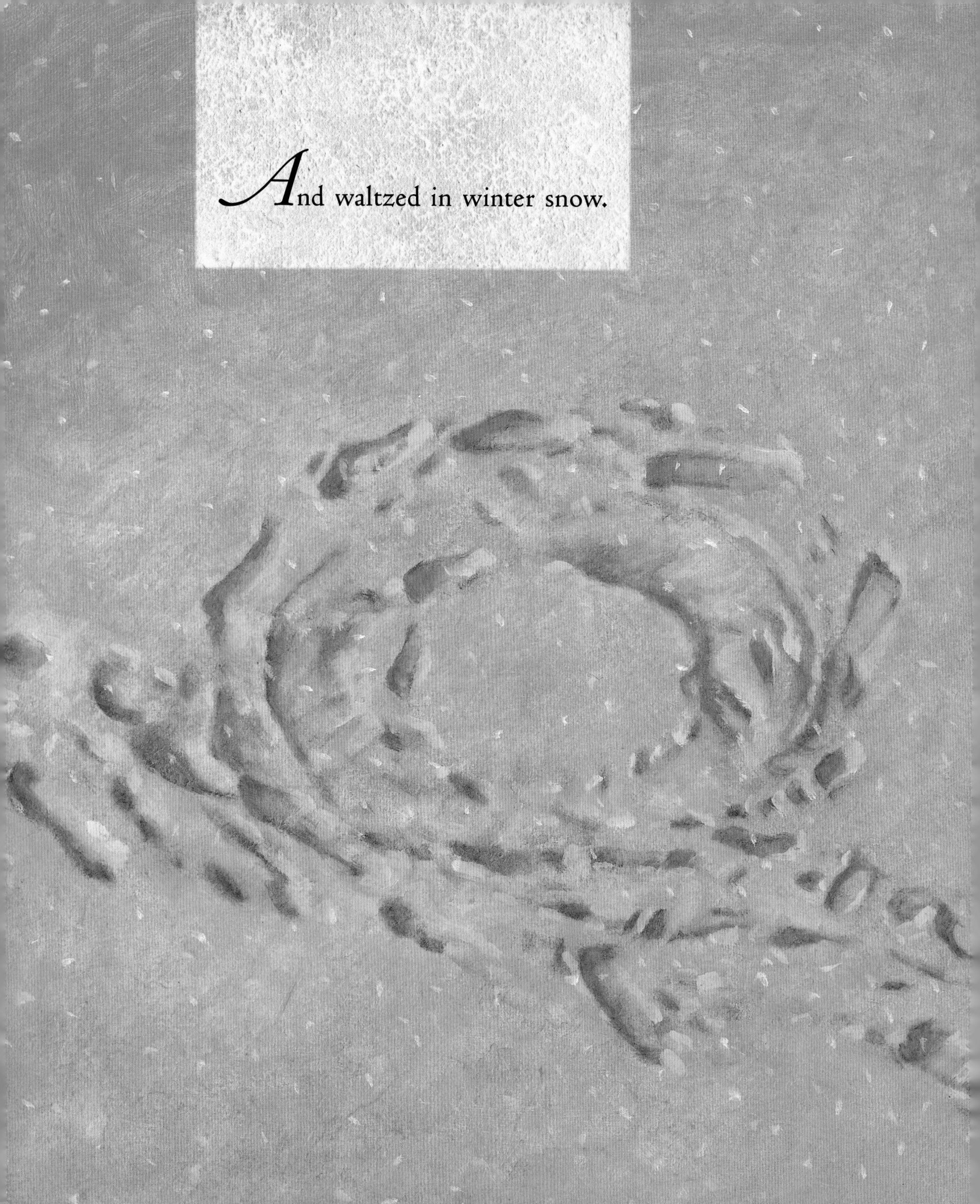

And waltzed in winter snow.

But now that I am old and grey,
My dancing nights are done.
I've chosen you, great-grandchild,
To take my place, so come...

Let me give you Tiger's hand –
The moon is rising high.
I'll sit and watch you dancing both,
Beneath the starbright sky.